Not Quite Dead Enough

Det. Lt. Andy Forbes knew this would be a rough case from the first call. The second and third confirmed the idea.

Contents

About the author

CD Moulton has traveled extensively over much of the world both in the music business, where he was a rock guitarist, songwriter and arranger and in an import/export business. He has been everything from a bar owner to auto salvage (junkyard) manager, longshoreman to high steel worker, orchid grower to landscaper, tropical fish farmer to commercial fisherman. He started writing books in 1983 and has published more than 350 books as of January 1, 2023. His most popular books to date are about research with orchids, though much of his science fiction and fantasy work has proven popular. He wrote the CD Grimes, PI series, and the Det. Nick Storie series, Clint Faraday series, and many other works.

He now resides in Gualaca, Chiriqui, Panamá, where he writes books, plays music with friends, does research with orchids and medicinal plants. He has lately become involved in fighting for the rights of the indigenous people, who are among his closest friends, and in fighting the extreme corruption in the courts and police in Panamá.

He offers the free e-book, *Fading Paradise*, that explains what he has been through because of the corruption.

CD is the discoverer of the Chadam Protocol for curing cancer.

Facebook page Ambrosia peruviana for cancer.

A Dream Date

Eileen McEvers looked out over the little lake and sighed. She leaned against her date's chest and nuzzled a bit, then ran her hand across his abdomen just above the belt buckle. He kissed her lightly. Her hand moved downward. The kiss became more intense.

They were alone here. There was no one for more than two miles. This was the dream date she had pictured so many times before, the one that would lead to a more permanent stay in paradise. She had worked so hard to get this one. He wasn't going to disappoint her like the others. She just knew that. This was special all the way. This was it! He was known to be very selective in who he would date and who he wouldn't. He was a private person. He had probably laid fifty women, as goodlooking and nice as he was, but he never talked about them. Ever. She had been close to brag sessions among the guys and he would never say anything. Gordon Gibbs, a sort of third choice at closing time type, had made fun of him once about him never having a story to tell.

She remembered the shocked look on Gord's

face when he got the answer! "Some people talk, some people do."

She unclasped the buckle and undid the button. He unsnapped her bra and lifted the blouse. It was more intense. He slipped his pants down, she dropped her underwear.

The kiss was hard enough to hurt a litttle. It was bliss multiplied. He was moving over her. She was welcoming him.

Then his hands were around her neck. What the Hell!? She couldn't breathe. She didn't want rough sex! It was too much! She was blacking out! This wasn't a sex game – he was killing her!

She tried to fight back, but was already too weak. Then dark cold blackness. Then nothing.

He sobbed and looked down at the body of this pretty girl. This one was too far.

His mother was dead! How could she be standing there, yelling in her strident voice that he was a no-good pervert who was going straight to Hell! She was responsible, but he was too! If he hadn't ended it, she would get pregnant and ruin both their lives! Thank God that could never happen now!

He could see and hear her. She was dead, but not quite dead enough. This girl was dead. She wouldn't come back to haunt him like his mother.

How he hated the woman who bore him! She was always there when anyone got close to him. She had always managed to make him back off before, but he was human! He needed some things in life! Now she was going stop him from getting them!

He couldn't go to the church. He was a bastard. The man he thought was his father wasn't. Mother told him that when he was eight years old and wanted to know why all his friends went to church, but he didn't. She showed him in the Bible that no bastard nor to his seventh descendent could enter the church.

He didn't believe in a God that would hold the child responsible for what his mother and father did. What? They could pray and be forgiven, but the child, who had nothing to do with it past being born, couldn't?

Not be forgiven. The child hadn't done any-thing.

"Be sure there's nothing that could identify you!" his mother demanded. "Put the body in those trees. Be sure you don't have anything of hers in the car. Wipe off the fingerprints. I made sure no one knows she came here with you. Get rid of that soda cup and the sandwich wrapper on the way back somewhere. It will have her DNA on it...."

She kept suggesting things, he did them. He was humiliated and scared. It was because of her, but he would have to pay if they found out.

There had to be a way to get her out of his life! This was too far! There had to be a way to exorcise the demon who was his mother from his life. There had to be! She was pure evil!

He had even used a branch to wipe out the tire marks and footprints around the table where he ... where he did it.

He wanted to die, but wasn't sure there was no Hell. He didn't believe in Heaven, but he had doubts about Hell. He was living in it since he was eight years old!

He drove slowly back to Vinceburg, nine miles from the lake. He didn't pass any cars until he was only about two miles away from home, when he turned onto the main road.

He went to the Moonlight Bar to order a strong Scotch and Soda. No one paid anymore attention to him than they ever had. He was known and was medium popular. He looked like his father, according to his mother, which meant women would be after him. Remember that a woman had one aim in life. To trap a man into taking care of her for life – like his father didn't do for her.

He had asked if that meant she was with his father to try to trap him. She slapped him so hard he had a mark on his face for more than a whole day!

How he hated her! He had to find a way to stop her from doing this to him!

He chatted for a few minutes with the guys about football, then went home to bed.

Detective Lieutenant Andrew Forbes, Violent Crimes, shoved the file into the drawer and sat back. That had been a mean one, but he did solve it. More than a year, watching and waiting. He found the likely killer, but didn't stop looking elsewhere. He was human. He could be wrong.

He hadn't been on that one. Frederick Bethampton was gone for life. He fully expected the death sentence to be mitigated. More than eighty percent of them were. He had done his job. This one was permanently off the streets. That's what counted.

Sarah Jenkins answered the 9-1-1 line and pointed to him. He took the call. A girl's body was found by the lake. Eileen McEvers, 21. Rather pretty. Tended to be a party girl, but not to the the extremes so many were.

He went to the car with Sarah, who was teamed with him this month. If a case came up they were teamed until it was solved or until they couldn't spend the shared time on it anymore.

Marty Harolds, the EMS driver, pointed to the wad of CSI people by some large oaks near the shore of the lake. He said it was a girl he'd met a couple of months ago on her twenty first. They got along. She was popular, but so were a lot of others. Seemed a normal type.

"You dated her?" Andy asked, mostly as a joke. Marty was reputed to date a lot of women.

"Depends on what you mean by 'dated,' huh, Marty?" Sarah asked.

Marty grinned and shrugged.

They went to look at the body. Not very much. An obvious strangulation.

Eva Manners, the head of the CSI team, said, "Fully dressed, but the blouse wasn't buttoned right and the panties were caught in a wrap, so that, at least, was put on her after death. It won't be rape. She was experienced. I knew her and gave her advice about some of the guys. Not an easy piece of ass, but not among the hardest, either.

"Tentatively, nine thirty to ten fifteen."

Andy nodded. He'd seen her around town with several different men. She liked the jock type.

There wasn't much to be found. It was obvious someone erased footprints and tire prints. There was no trash in the area. There was none in the bins. They were emptied three times per week and not many came out here. They would in a month, when the weather was warm enough for enjoying the lake.

"Sarah! We may have a minor break!" Eva called. "There's what appears to be a pubic hair caught under her fingernail. No DNA. No follicle, but we may find something from it."

"Ten four. Every little bit is a little bit."

They checked around the area, then headed back to the station. They would have to find where she was yesterday. They might get a break. She might have told someone who she was dating last night.

"I'll get in touch with her parents. Mother. Father left three years ago, ostensibly for a job in Nashville. Comes back about three times a year. Mother on Willow Road. Box one seventy four."

"We can go out there. Maybe she kept a diary or datebook or something. I've met the mother. Very religious type. This will hit her hard. Only child.

They drove out to find Flo Hern and Ed Macon there. Those two were the people in the station who handled bad news and contacting next of kin and such. They were with a slightly plump woman in her early forties. She was in shock and confused. Sarah said they had to try to find things among the things Eileen left. Perhaps they should come back later. Flo explained. Mrs. McEvers couldn't understand anything about it. She said to go where they had to and do what they had to do. It didn't matter anymore. Nothing did. She broke down.

Andy never knew what to do in those situations. Sarah wasn't a lot better. Flo waved them inside. She said Eileen's bedroom was second on the right in the hall.

The bedroom was neat and clean. There were several pictures on the dresser. Sarah and Andy recognized all of them as people around town. Most were signed. Sarah made a list:

John Norton
Robert James
Rita Sanchez
Marty Harolds
Bill Betts
Donna Redding
Diana Downs
George Fender
Steve Owens

She had an album with the same ones and several others. Hopefully, one or more could tell them something.

She hadn't kept a diary that they could find. She had a computer, which was where Sarah said she kept personal notes in a coded section, but Eileen didn't use the computer much. Some e-mails and a few downloaded movies. Romantic things. Slightly erotic, but a long way from porno.

Sarah checked the history. There was nothing.

They went back out front, where Mrs. McEvers was a little better. She said Eileen was a good girl. She was a little wild, but all girls are at that age. She had been, but she found God understood and didn't hold youthful transgressions against anyone when they finally saw the light.

"Flo, she would go to bars sometimes, but she would only have one beer. She saw what alcohol did to her uncle and almost to her father. She read something that said it was genetic. If your parents are subject to alcoholism, you will be. She was very careful. She knew I drank a bit when I was younger and that it never got a hold on me. I'm genetically resistant. Her father isn't. She said she could hope she got my genes, but she was not going to take chances.

"I suppose she was no virgin. I wasn't. I never asked.

"I worried because she was too romantic. She didn't see what was chemistry. She thought she was in love every week when she was sixteen and seventeen, but it was moderated. She knew it was just chemistry, but I think she did feel she had found someone special, though she wouldn't talk about it. The last week she was on cloud nine. It was because of the date she had last night.

"She wouldn't tell me who. She said it would wait until she was sure on a real basis, not just hormones."

"She dated the men in the pictures on her dresser?" Sarah asked.

"She dated some of them and just hung around with the others. She did say there were a couple of possibilities of something more permanent, that they were all dreams walking. Robert was one she said there could be something more with. He's a very sweet man. He respects others and they respect him. He's big enough that no one will try to walk all over him. She really liked Steve, but he was cool to the idea of getting very close to anyone.

"The girls were her closest, you know. Pals. Shared all the secrets and giggled. I did that. I made up some of the secrets, but we all do. We want to sound more worldly than we are.

"That's before we understand how cruel the world can be."

They chatted for another half hour. They didn't learn much more than that, but it could be a lot.

They went into town and found where John Norton was a mechanic at Wally's Motors. He was saddened about Eileen. He was 26, but she had wanted to date him. He waited until she was of age. They did the sex bit sometimes, but as close friends, not as lovers. She could be clinging, but would back off when someone told her it was getting to be too much. He was with the guys at work at the Happy Hour bar until about ten thirty.

Diana Downs, a friend of both of them, had handled that for him. She had started to apologize. He told her it happened. See it for what it was and don't let it get to you. She had later thanked him for it when she almost ran another person away because of it. Donna. another friend, had told her because he said she was going to make a good friend into an enemy. They all got along very well, now.

Diana and Donna had 2-D's fashions. It was a small shop that found what was popular and found it at good prices. They weren't getting rich, but they were doing alright. They closed the shop for the day when they heard about Eileen. They were close.

Sarah asked if they knew anything about who Eileen dated last night. They didn't. They said she was being mysterious, that it was someone they all loved. She seemed to think they had both dated this guy, but didn't have a clue, other than that. They all dated a lot of the same people.

Bill Betts was a driver for a trucking company. He was in town a lot of the time, but was statewide. He had been in Sandervale last night. He supposed Eileen dated all the guys.

They knew Marty. He would have been first to

tell them anything he knew.

Rita Sanchez was hostess at Pedro's House of Pizza. They joked about a Mexican having an Italian restaurant. She pointed out that pizza was tomato pie, from Chicago, not Italy. Spaghetti came from China and pizza came from Chicago. The most popular Italian foods weren't Italian.

She didn't know who Eileen was with last night. She hadn't seen her since last Saturday. Everybody dated almost everybody in their little clique.

Robert James was a watchmaker. He looked like a running back. He was a mild-mannered person with a great sense of humor. He was a little broken up about Eileen. He had once considered marrying her – if he got around to marrying anyone. She would be like her mother. A very good person. He had no idea who she was dating now. He was with Lorene Sampson at her place until about twelve thirty.

George Fender was a musician. Heavy metal rock. Writer and arranger. Fairly good voice for rock, excellent drummer and keyboardist, some rhythm guitar. Played bass.

To make a living, he did landscaping, which he held a degree in. He was a little serious about Eileen a few months ago, but it blew over for both of them. They were both too possessive and knew it. Life would be a competition, and life like that wasn't worth the trouble. They could romp now and then until one or both met the right one, then would both be down the line. It was what they believed.

"We both believe, no promises, no problem. Once you make the commitment, you're slime if you break it."

He was in the studio until two in the morning or so. He didn't pay much attention to time when he was working the music bit.

Steve Owens was a strange type. He was open and affable, but very private. He said he hadn't dated any of the girls. He didn't date women often. They got the idea he was gay or bi. He was with friends until about nine, then went home. He stopped at Fancy's for one drink about nine fifteen. Gerry Slocum was there.

That was the list. Back to the station. Both Sarah and Andy liked all of that group. It would be a crying shame if one was a killer!

"We can trace where she was earlier yesterday, but no one knew where she was last night or with whom," Sarah suggested. "Her mother said she was at the house until after seven, so it's only a couple of hours. Surely, someone saw her."

"She didn't drink. She had a date, so wouldn't be at a bar. She would have left the house only a short time before the date," Andy said. "I would say ... she was dating someone who worked regular hours. She went somewhere while he SSS'ed, then they drove out to the lake."

"A little café-type restaurant or a soda shop kind of thing."

"It'll be a break. It will be close to where he lives."

"Except for the fact everything's close to everything else here. Eastpoint and Millerton are the farthest, one on one side, the other on the other. Two miles. A bit distant for walking.

"What if she took a cab?"

"Three of them." He called. She wasn't a rider anywhere last night.

Sarah thought a minute. "Sandy's, MacDonald's, TGIF, KFC. TGIF and KFC are a bit more expensive. MacDonald's is a hangout for teen-agers, mostly. Let's try Sandy's first."

They drove to the popular coffee house. Eileen had been there for about half an hour. No one noticed when she left. No one saw her with anyone.

"So. We have to find who ... damn!" Sarah complained. "A couple hundred live in this area!"

"*She* lived in this area, meaning someone could have driven to pick her up from anywhere. This is going to be a mean one."

Donna Redding was a bit excited. She had wanted to date this guy for months. He seemed to always have a date, but tonight would be the night. She was going to see if he was half as good as she knew he would be. He was the type you got serious over.

Well, she was twenty six. Maybe it was about time she thought about getting serious. She didn't believe in starting a family too young, but young enough to where you can enjoy it.

She was ditzo! A date, and she was thinking about marriage? Would that turn any guy off so fast you wouldn't know which way was up, or what?! Start thinking like that and tonight's a guaranteed disaster!

She had to close the shop tonight. Diana would come in if she called her, but that wouldn't be fair. Nine wasn't that late. He would pick her up when she closed.

She was on pins and needles. This guy dated everyone, so she had to be special. He was quiet. He would be the slow and sensual kind. Not the heat and passion type.

Great! She was, too!

She thought nine would never come. Of course, a customer came in ten minutes before closing. She would probably hang around until ten and decide to decide tomorrow or something.

She lucked out! The woman had seen a dress in the window exactly like the one she had five years ago. If they had her size, sold!

They had her size. The one in the window. She left at nine oh two. Donna closed and went out to the waiting car. She had managed to change and fix herself up before the customer came in. They had a changing room and shower right there in the shop.

He was a dream! He thought of everything!

"I figured you would be hungry. We said no fancy restaurants or any of that. This is just to get to know each other better.

"Shrimp in a basket? I've seen you going for seafood."

"I've died and gone to heaven! I love these Cajun shrimp! I just love them!"

They drove out to Flint River and parked in a private little spot with a clear view of the scenic winding river. There was a full moon that brought everything to as close to perfection as she could think.

After an hour of talking and moving closer and

closer on the little grassy knoll, she leaned against him and said he was a dream. He respected her. He was a gentleman.

They got closer and closer. It was going to happen, as they both knew it would. He had his shirt off and she had gotten rid of some things. He held her close. He was kissing her neck and her blouse was off and she was going to explode. She laid back and clung to him. He reached to pull her mouth to his. She ran her hand down.

What the Hell!? Let go! I can't breathe! I don't want this kind of ... oh, God! I can't ... can't... oh, no!

He laid her gently back and sobbed.

"Well? Didn't I *tell* you she would? Didn't I? Well?" his mother screeched. "Oh, but she's *different*! She's not *like* that!

"They all are! You're pure stupid to think anyone's any different! You're a sick pervert, just like your father!"

"Leave me alone, you damned witch!" he screamed.

"I'll never leave you alone! You're just like your father! You *know* what he did to me!"

"You got pregnant to trap him into marrying you, then he wouldn't, and *he's* a sick pervert? What are you? I hate your damned guts! He didn't do anything to you! You did it to yourself!"

"You'll pay for treating me like this! You damned perverted little *bastard*!"

It was hopeless. He got rid of anything that could identify him. He placed the body between some large rocks and went back to town. He stopped at the bar and talked with the guys for a few minutes, said he was on the early shift tomorrow, and went home.

This had to end. It simply had to end. He couldn't go on this way.

It was over a month since Eileen McEvers. They had made zero progress since that first two days. Sarah was going to another partner in three days.

Andy shoved the notes and pages of interviews into their envelope and sat back to think.

His line buzzed. It was another strangling.

Sarah was at the café down the block. He called her and said he'd pick her up. It looked like another case for them that was really part of the McEvers thing.

Sarah bought her clothes at the shop. She was shocked and surprised that Donna would go out there with anyone she didn't know very well, indeed. She was definitely not promiscuous.

Stupid! It was one of that group.

Eva said this was a bit strange. If it was set up to make it look like a sexual thing, whoever was good at it, except it was damned unlikely that McEvers had sexual relations before her death and Redding definitely didn't.

"Ten to ten thirty last night."

Andy looked thoughtful. He said he read a thing in a psychology book about a type of killer. They would get into a sexual situation, but the completion of the act, for the man, was killing the woman. The regular things that they found the evidence of here was foreplay. This was looking like that kind of thing. The man in the psychological studies was impotent.

"Are you thinking what I'm thinking?" Sarah asked. "Owens? Not actually gay. Impotent. Frustrated."

"I wasn't thinking of anyone, but you're right. We have to find where everyone was on two nights.

"Sarah, our killer has a car or small truck. He's strong. He's able to project ... well, maybe not. Maybe he's sincere, but is so frustrated at the critical moment he reacts.

"The study said frustration and uncontrollable rage. What this lacks is the evidence that was always there of rage. This is almost a quiet.... The way they were laid out seems to show something other than rage. It doesn't make any sense.

"I've studied this kind of thing a lot. What about if he thinks he's possessed? He goes with a girl in all innocence, then is caught in a mental trap where a demon takes over. When it's over, he tries to show his respect by making the body look like everything was proper.

"That would mean a super-religious influence and conflict. We have to know if any of them had a childhood with one parent religious and the other antireligious.

"Our clues are too mixed. We can't get anywhere with this the way we're going. It's mostly a feeling, but I think this is a case where the psychobabble is more or less the case."

"You went into that more than I did. I did look for a nutcase type of thing, but those signs are usually clear enough. The rage isn't here. That's where the mutilation killings come in. No sign of it. No one is taunting us, but that could come later if it turns serial.

"I read a few possession things. This fits that more than direct schizoid reaction, I think.

"On the other hand, it doesn't fit at all. It was too planned. It was too careful about clues and evidence. There was a lot of thought before the killing.

"Let's find where everyone was last night. This time, we check it to the Nth degree. Someone was not where they said they were before.

"First, which ones have cars?"

Andy checked his list on his notebook computer. "Norton, James, Betts, Fender, Owens. All of them."

"Shit! Not even one elimination!"

"One, but he was never in it. Marty."

"But he has use of a car. He's twenty four hours on duty. No eliminations."

Eva said she was about through. Her crew would comb the area, but there was nothing except some candy wrappers and soda cans and such. She noted that the grass on a little knoll was crushed a bit, so that was probably where they sat. It would get special attention.

The headed back to the car. Marty came to the van. He dropped a limeade soda can into the trash bin on the van, then grinned. "I didn't leave any evidence to screw things up. It never left my hand since I got it.

"I'm not supposed to eat or drink anything. I haven't had anything since the call woke me up. What the hell. I wish it was a gallon of strong coffee!"

They laughed. Marty went to help Eva and they got in the car and headed for the office.

Norton was out. This time, he spent the night with Yvonne Helton. He had been there all night. She would know the instant he got out of bed. He got up twice to piss. Eat your heart out! (To Sarah, who grinned.)

Robert James was with Rita Sanchez until about midnight.

Bill Betts was at the Starlighter until after ten.

This time, they checked each one out. He was.

George Fender was home. He was in.

Steve Owens was in and out of several places. There were periods of almost an hour he couldn't account for with proof.

"Fender and Owens. I don't believe either did it," Sarah said. Andy agreed.

"That means we're looking for someone from outside that group, which makes this meaner and meaner," Sarah complained. "On the other hand, I'm glad none of our group is a killer."

Andy looked thoughtful.

"Well, a week and nothing new except Eva says she has prelim pictures that show something may have ended up missing from the Redding scene. It's something that shouldn't be important, but she noted it. A piece of trash. Maybe the wind blew it away.

"I may have something to check out that could connect. Gladys Vernon said a man tried to get her to go to the lake with him last night. Fancy car. BMW. Handsome and seemed nice, but those two women were murdered and she was scared.. The license plate started with D2B. Black."

"She can describe him?"

"He was in the car, but he was probably six feet or more and had a good build and brown wavy hair and eyes and perfect teeth and wore a gold watch and a ring with a ruby in onyx and a shirt with the Polo logo on it and was maybe twenty five years old.

"She would notice all that. She was tempted because he was handsome and rich and very nice.

"Gladys makes a few bucks on the side from her waitress job."

Andy went to the computer to check the license plate numbers that started with D2B. There were 999 of them. Seven were for BMW's.

He wrote down the seven and addresses. Four would wait. Three were within two hours driving time of town. One was in town. Mike Little.

Mike Little was 49 years old. Not him.

"Kid about twenty five?"

"Andy checked. Yeah. Girl. Anne Marie. Son twenty two, married, living in Napa Valley, California."

Next closest was only thirty six miles away. Valleton. Daniel Hampton. 28. Owned a gymnasium and a boxing instruction studio and karate ditto.

Andy found the number of the gymnasium from the web address. He called and was given a roaming cell number. Hampton answered and said he was there and that he saw two pretty girls he tried to pick up, but it was no go.

Andy thanked him and rang off.

"I think maybe I want to see if that BMW was in the area on two specific dates. I want to know a thing or two about Daniel Hampton."

Sarah more than agreed with that. Maybe they finally had a break. Neither believed they would get one in this case, but it was fifty-fifty. Maybe it paid off! It was time something did!

"Valleton. I know their force. Just four cops. No problem with cooperation," Sarah said. "Let's run over. I have my rotation set up, but I'll be available for this case on an as-needed basis. I am interested in it."

They got an off area duty form. Andy said he was going to check on a few things there before they went to Valleton. He went to the nine filling stations in the area. No one remembered any such BMW in the last couple of days or nights. They had too many others to be able to check back earlier. If the driver used a card it would be easy to check.

The man at the Texaco station ran a computer check to find a card for that person. He didn't have one, but used a Visa card to purchase gasoline and maintenance. That meant he could use any station.

Andy got the card number and went back to the office. He went through Judge Williams for a discreet court order to Visa on use of that card for the past six months. The information was sent by secure computer link (Yeah, right) directly to Williams' chambers.

Nothing that would eliminate Hampton. He hadn't used the card on any date that interested them. It wouldn't put him there, but it didn't put him not there.

Andy sighed and they headed for Valleton. It was, at least, a scenic ride.

Four hours in Valleton. They checked what they could, but were getting a little frustrated when Sarah suggested that Hampton owned a karate studio. They had statewide competition the night Redding was killed.

Andy checked the schedule of the matches. Hampton faced Ebert at eight and Franconi at nine. He was definitely there. He took the gold (plated) medal for the matches.

They headed back to the station.

"That highway led to a fast dead end!" Andy remarked.

Sarah gave him the finger. "At least it got us away from town for a day."

"There's that."

Steve Owens went to the bar for another 7-7. He looked around, spotted a familiar face, and went to say, "Hello! I don't think I've ever seen you here."

"Oh, hi, Steve. I was passing and always heard about this being a swinger bar. I was a bit curious.

"You aren't married. You swing?"

"A little. I'm bi, but you figured I'm mostly gay years ago.

"This place is just open. It's not gay or swingers or heteros or S and M or anything. It's all of it. The rule is that, if you're prejudiced about anything – except pedophiles. Nobody accepts pedophiles here or anywhere else I know of – there are other bars where you'll be welcome. This ain't one of them.

"You're a living doll. You'll get propositions here in the dozens. Don't take offense, okay?"

"Why would I? It's sort of a trip when you know a lot of people want you. It's the way the world is. In my profession we have to study a lot about human nature. I think most of that's genetic. Why hold it against someone because they like rice and you like potatoes or that they have brown eyes and yours are blue?"

"I didn't think you'd go for anything, would you? Hint! Hint!"

He laughed. "I don't know, really. I never had any experience. My mother watched me like a hawk. Pop preached about the evil people in the world who would want to seduce me and lead me straight to Hell. I know I wouldn't be interested in some things. I would maybe like to see what some things are like, but only from my end of the stick, so to speak.

"I have nothing against it. Freddie Cox is a friend. He wanted to do things, but he doesn't appeal to me. Fat women turn me off. I think fat anything does, and Freddie is fat."

"I'm not!"

He laughed again. "No, you and I have almost identical builds."

"Seriously, if you ever want to experiment or anything, I'm right here, and I do very much want you. You're clean and have a great personality and care about your friends. The thing I worry about is getting too serious with someone like you. That can't work for long when one is straight and the other gay. You should have kids. You have great genetics. That should be passed on.

"That's my dilemma. I have great genes, but I

don't want to be tied down in a marriage. I can't change what I am. It's just there. It wouldn't be fair to the woman.

"I do like a romp every once in awhile with a woman, but it's for fun and maybe communication. No more."

"You're honest about it. I think maybe you would be fun. I care about you, about all of our group. I don't care for the love bit. Not the passionate romantic 'I can't live without you!' bullshit."

"I'm here and available and anxious."

"I don't know. I've never done any of that. I don't have the experience all of you think I do."

"No one could survive what we like to fantasize about you. You wouldn't have time to get over the first before the next fifty were all over you. You do have a lot of experience. That comes with looking like you and having your personality."

"I don't have all that experience. It's bullshit.

"Let's don't talk about that. I'm private about what I do. I don't want to do anything with anyone who's not. That isn't right. Who you share your body with is personal and private. Period."

"You're a lot deeper than I would have thought. You're a very good person."

"No, I'm not. I try to be what I want other people to be. That's all. I want to understand me, and it just doesn't work, sometimes. It's easier to understand someone else. I don't know why ... a lot of things."

They talked about philosophy for awhile. Steve would meet him later. He knew a place he could use, a friend's place. The friend was on vacation in San Francisco and wouldn't be back for several days. It would be private and personal.

"This is a beautiful place. I heard Milt was gay. It's really as good a view as we have."

"Milt's not gay, but he likes a romp now and then. We've been friends for a long time. We don't ... I won't talk about that. Neither of us accept sex as less than private, but I will say Milt is like you. It's from only one end.

"You're an affectionate person, by nature. You're holding back when you don't want to.

"Are you worried that you might like this too much, that it means you're latent?"

"No. Not really. I just don't want to let ... I want ... I don't really know. I want to be free, but I don't think I can ever be. I'm really screwed up, Steve. You don't know how much. I don't want to live like this anymore. I really don't have control of anything in my life.

"Damn it! I want to be able to hold another person without being afraid of what it will bring!

I thought maybe I could hold you and care, but she isn't going to let me! I know it!

"Steve, I'm crazy. I have to be.

"Steve, let me explain. You're strong enough that you can stop me. Don't let me get anywhere I can get a knife or gun or anything. I think she could make me use it.

"It's my mother. She's dead, but she haunts me. She's not dead enough! Oh, God!"

Andy sat back and thought. There was something he had seen. Or heard. It was a major clue.

It was nagging at the back of his mind. He knew he knew something, but couldn't bring it out.

He went through the short list. Nothing. His clues weren't going to lead anywhere if he couldn't find a connection. This kind of thing too often didn't have any connection. Not that a sane person could understand.

He was coming around to believing insanity was behind it.

Okay. Side notes. Was anything there?

He remembered something Sarah said. He called her and asked about the bit of trash that had been in a picture and had ended up missing. What was it?

"Let me check. It's in this file. Redding.

"A bottle or can by where the body was found.

Green. It was gone when we started collecting things in bags.

"Andy, it was windy out there. It could have been a piece of green cellophane. It can be the exact colors on cans and bottles. I noted it because I never miss that kind of thing. It was probably nothing. I doubt we could get anything from it, other than maybe prints we don't have a match for – and that probably didn't have a damned thing to do with the case."

"No. I think maybe you just gave me the solution. I have to check a few things out, but ... damn! I like him!"

He chatted a minute, then went to the cabinet to take out a file. It was seriously lacking, being arrest record (none), driver's license, work record, social security and insurance information, and the normal age-sex-features thing.

He went to the secondary files. What they had on general information didn't add much. Born, mother, father, mother divorced – lost case because DNA showed father wasn't father. Only issue, son, eight at the time. Some psychological issues.

There was a single reference. A woman from Children's Services for the state had worked for a bit with the son since he was seven years old and displayed certain disturbing traits.

Amanda Fischer.

He called the number and spoke with the supervisor. Amanda had retired last year, but she had the contact number. He would be able to discuss what wasn't restricted confidential information.

He called Amanda. She said she vaguely remembered the case. Very sad. Mother a control freak and father somewhat extreme in religious matters. Mother was bitter and took her hatred of men out on her son. There was evidence that she was telling the boy that women were evil things who would cause him to go to hell if he fell for their lies and charms. He seemed to be strong enough to recover from whatever was behind it.

"Andy, I remember a little more. The father was a religious nut, but the son didn't attend any church. Mother was semi-religious, but never went to church since her son was born. The boy was obviously going to be very handsome, which the supposed father was not. That's what eventually led to the father demanding DNA tests as a way to get away from the mother. He was successful there.

"If I remember, the mother got married again. She intensely hated men, but kept getting married, more as a spite thing against other women. It seemed, from remarks and things she did, that she hated other women even more than she hated men. All husbands and a couple of men she went after said she was a schemer who wanted to run their lives. You couldn't believe anything she said. They all also said it was important to get that boy away from her, but there was never any action for that, sad to say. It was all lost in the bureaucracy.

"I'll go down to the office and get the files. I'll release them to you if you can give a valid reason to have them."

"You heard about the two women who were strangled?"

"So. I'm so sorry. I wish I'd had the training to help that boy. I felt there was something very heavy on his shoulders, but he wasn't communicative. I understand he has the sociopathic ability to make people – I don't believe that, but he may have developed an ability. He was naturally an outgoing sort of boy. He was in deep need of someone who cared. His father – stepfather – did, but abandoned the boy to get away from the mother.

Andy agreed to meet her at records at the courthouse. She went through the files and said the mother had restricted information as long as she was alive. She was dead. She would give him the file, or copy it for him.

He took the files back to the station and put the coffee urn on. This was going to take hours, but he had to be right.

The first was birth records and marriage certificates and such. It started as a normal sort of thing. The mother was said to be a bit antisocial, but overcame it. The father seemed to think she had become pregnant to trap him, but he was religious and said the sin was his, so he would pay what the lord considered to be his debt and responsibility.

The first file was when the boy was seven. He showed some signs of abuse in school and the teacher had referred the case to Amanda. She found the methods the mother used to control the boy were borderline and counseled that she would bring action if the mother didn't moderate her discipline.

When the boy was eight, he became depressed and kept saying he was going to Hell because God was a monster who punished innocent people for things they had no guilt for. He punsihed the victim and let the sinners off for a few dollars or a few hail Mary's or less. The mother said it was because the father was causing all kinds of problems, not her. The DNA and divorce came a month later. The father tried to get custody of the boy, but the mother was the natural mother. She contested and won.

"I wonder if you would be a very different person if he had won, or if he would do the same things to you in the name of religion. Religion seems to be behind it or a huge part of it," Andy murmured.

The next file was about the next husband, who never was close to the boy, and the next, who tried to get close to him, but was rejected.

The mother became more and more a control freak and controlled the boy far too much, but he was seventeen by that time and would be away from her soon.

And she died two years ago, when you were twenty three. She had some kind of hold on you until then. Your mother didn't hate men half so much as she hated women. You were brainwashed by that thing, then she was gone. Now you're a killer. I wonder if you have any control at all in that.

He sighed and sat back.

His desk phone rang. It was a call direct to him.

"Andy? Steve Owens here. I have to discuss some things with you. It's about the strangulation murders. The one who did them is here with me. You have to hear his story and understand. He's not responsible. Really. I know that."

"Marty Harolds?"

"You knew? When?"

"About an hour ago. I may be able to understand a lot about it. I have the records from when he was seven and his mother was destroying his life."

"I think he's schizophrenic. I actually talked with his mother. She's in possession of part of his mind."

Andy heard a high strident voice swearing and accusing men for all her problems and she was going to get even! There was a small sound of a scuffle and a muted murmur, then sobs.

"I'm holding Marty. She has no power if I hold him.

"Andy, we have to do something, but I can't begin to know how or what."

"Where are you? I'll come."

"Milt Starr's place."

"Twenty minutes. You'll be alright until then?"

"Nothing's alright. I can hold him. I'd like to hold him for more than twenty minutes."

"Be there."

Andy shoved the records into his drawer, locked it, and headed for the car. This was weird. He wished Sarah was there, then was glad she wasn't. He didn't think she was equipped to handle what was about to go down. He doubted that Father Grimes, at the Catholic church, could handle what must basically become an exorcism.

He went into the house and through to the entertainment room. Steve Owens was there with Marty in his arms. Marty seemed to be asleep.

"He's finally relaxed enough to sleep. Let's allow him sleep as long as we can. You can't believe the Hell he's lived with for most of his life," Steve said very quietly.

"I've studied a lot of it. There are huge gaps. I can't begin to understand how he managed to not go to church when his father was so religious. The mother had been religious at the time, so why wasn't he ever in church?"

"His mother wouldn't allow it. He's a bastard and was told none to his seventh descendant could enter the church.

"Can you picture a mother who would tell her

own son such a thing?"

"I can't picture a lot about this one. I gathered there was something like that because of his remarks to a social worker that God was a monster who punished people for things they weren't guilty of and let the real sinners say a hail Mary or two and get away with it."

"Whatever the mechanism, he really is possessed. That won't hold in law. We have to find a way to help him. He's a good person, despite what's happened. I can't believe the strength of a person to hold out against that for so long. He wants to die, but is positive he goes to hell, no matter what."

"I looked up some of what she told him about bastards. The Bible doesn't say, anywhere, that they will go to Hell. It only says they can't enter the church. I think I can convince him of that – but not if it means he suicides."

"The Bible does say suicides go to Hell."

"Then the rest of his life is agony. There's no way to turn in that. Any way it goes, he's doomed to living in Hell for as long as he lives."

"Are you religious, Andy?"

"Depends on what you mean. The crap from the organized churches? No way! It's crap!"

"I'm not either.

"Maybe we can work something out. I want to

get rid of Mother Dearest."

Marty didn't wake up, but was struggling. Steve said she heard everything and was going to be a real fight.

Andy got an idea. He winked at Steve.

"Steve, the way I see this is that Mama knows perfectly damned well she's headed straight for the deepest depths of Hell. Don't pass go and don't collect two hundred dollars. She possessed him when she died to keep her spirit here.

"She's a spiteful monster. She's also stupid. She cut off her one way to continue here. If Marty has no children, who can she possess when he gets older and dies? Marty will be free, but she'll be burning in the lowest depths of Hell for eternity. I studied the works of Pope Pius the third or something such and the Borgias.

"There are four basic types of possession by a person who dies. Easiest and most common, though none are actually common, is through direct family descendants. Once started, that can't be altered. It can continue to the end of the family line.

"With someone like Marty, with the personality and good looks that are genetic dominants, there would probably have been descendants until the race dies out. She's made sure he won't have any descendants, so she goes to Hell the minute he dies. That comes from the old saw about a little knowledge being a dangerous thing. She could possess him, but that's a dead end because of what she is and what she's caused.

"I think we can get rid of her. Exorcize her. I also learned a lot about that in my study of what Popes Justinian and Claudius determined. It takes a few little things and concentration.

"It isn't Jesus or any saint who exorcizes. It's the ones doing the exorcism. If they're strong and concerted, they can overcome the demon. You've already proven you're stronger, and I'm not as strong, but we can't be resisted by anyone so stupid as not to study what she was doing all the way. She won't be able to thwart the eighth step. We'll have her in Hell within two hours, at most."

Steve gave him a look like Marty wasn't the only crazy one here. He raised an eyebrow.

"Let her talk. Keep close. You already proved you can stop her anytime you like."

Steve lightly shook Marty to wake him. He looked into his eyes and pushed him away just a bit. Marty's eyes were pleading.

"Mrs. Owens – or whatever name you're using – you might as well talk to me. Don't rant and rave. It will only hurt you."

"You don't scare me!" in a strident screeching voice.

"Stop yelling! You don't impress anyone with that crap!

"In the name of the almighty and St. Swithens, I demand you moderate your tones. You will answer me truthfully or you will find your journey to your fate much faster than you would wish, I guarantee you!"

"I don't believe you know anything! Who cares what some pope said who died a thousand years ago? I'm here and I'll stay here as long as I like!" It was still acid and strident, but the volume was down to almost normal.

"Step one. Completed. Demon knows she has limited power, so will, if intelligent, take into consideration what her actions will bring.

"You will tell me exactly why you have chosen the evil path here. You will tell me why such a thing as you would use her own flesh and blood in some ridiculous unthought-out scheme! Now!"

"I'll tell you nothing! You're one of them!"

Andy made some signs, then the sign of the cross.

"Ungh! Eh-eh-eh. Grng." Marty was struggling. Andy signed to Steve to hold him. Steve did. The struggles stopped. Andy signed to let Marty go a little.

"Talk or end you?"

"Bastard! Evil slime! unghhh! I'll ... unghh."

"Answer! Now!"

"His father did this to me! I will get even for that! He should have married me! We could have a good life! He cheated me out of my life!"

"Step two. Completed. Subject has stated unlogical thinking.

"Did you, or did you not, become pregnant for the sole purpose of entrapping Marty's father into supporting you for the rest of your life, and did you or did you not marry the man who thought he was the father for that same end?"

"I didn't ... you stinking bastard! You're all alike!"

"Answer! Now!" He signed for Steve to draw Marty closer, just a little. He did.

"Yes! But that is what all women do! It is what my mother did and her mother!"

"Step three. Completed. Subject has confessed it was not the fault of the father, it was the fault of herself that she has become what she has become.

"And you know the line about a bastard and his seventh descendant was rejected in the new testament as false. You used only the rejected part to try to turn your own flesh and blood into what you almost were able to do! True?"

"The Bible does say that!"

"And that part has been decreed not in force by God. You knew that, didn't you?"

"No! It is in the Bible!" She sounded confused and doubtful. The stridency was past. She was almost wailing.

"Admit the truth! Now!"

"It is the truth ... but maybe I didn't know about ... it is true."

"Steps four, five and six completed. Subject was deliberately using partial information. Subject admits there was no such stricture. Subject is aware she has failed.

"You are aware truth makes you weak and vulnerable. You are aware that you have no strength to resist me further, and that Steve has more strength and will work with me in all things.

"Step seven completed. Subject cannot resist step eight.

"Steve, stay close, but release all contact with Marty when I say.

"Marty, can you hear me?"

Marty struggled a bit, then said, in a clear voice, "You did it! Yes! I hear!"

"Marty. It is not over. There will be a struggle. She must go directly to Hell, but you will be free. You must join this part. Demand that she removes herself from your body when I make the sign. This will be painful, but it will be over."

He was looking around the room while talking. Steve asked what he wanted.

"A silver cross. I saw one somewhere."

"On the candlestick. There are two of them on the mantel."

He took the two silver candle holders and handed one to Steve. "Hold this between yourself and Marty. I will hold this between us, but will touch Marty on the forehead with it. She cannot jump to you or to me. There is no one else. She must leave Marty. She will be in Hell in ten!" (He signed for Steve to step away from Marty) "Nine!" (Marty screamed in the strident voice) "Eight!" (Marty started to run.) Andy yelled, "Marty! Resist! She doesn't have the strength to fight all of us!" (Marty fell to the floor and rolled around a bit.) "Seven!" (Marty tried to crawl toward the door.) "Six!" (Marty was screaming and sobbing.) "Five!" (Marty was jerking and gasping.) "Four!" (Marty was gibbering in terror.) "Three!" (Andy moved toward Marty.) "Two!" (The strident screech, "No! No! No!") "One!" (Andy placed the cross on the candlestick on Marty's forehead. Marty screamed and passed out.)

They sat close together. Steve held Marty and rocked him. There was a red burn of a cross on Marty's forehead. Andy knew that was psychosomatic. He had actually pulled off an exorcism! He did it all on the spur of the moment. He thought he should have said five or six steps, but had said eight, so had to come up with eight.

He had looked up a few things about exorcisms. He had quoted popes and such that didn't exist, but Marty wouldn't know that.

"She is burning in Hell. She was evil incarnate," Steve said to Marty. "You are one strong dude. Anyone else would have croaked years ago." He squeezed Marty's shoulders. Marty clung to him.

"This is the first time I remember ever holding anyone this way. I didn't make Hell. I'm in heaven.

"She's gone. There's a cold empty spot that's shrinking.

"What now? I killed those two women. I know the law won't believe it wasn't me, but it wasn't."

"We know that. We'll see what we can do. It's out of you. It won't happen again," Andy said. "I'll have to take you in, but to the hospital. For observation."

"Before that cross fades from your forehead," Steve said.

They went to the cars. Marty rode with Steve to the hospital, where the doctors checked him over. He was diagnosed with severe exhaustion and a second degree burn. The doctors couldn't explain why there was no cellular damage except directly where the cross was showing. It would probably leave a very faint permanent scar.

Andy went back to the station to file the report. He asked that Marty be released on his own recognizance, which Judge Williams couldn't understand. You don't release a double murderer on anyone's recognizance!

Andy called Ed Levin, the only lawyer he had a true respect for in town, and had him accept responsibility.

Then they all went home. Marty would have to be at work in the morning if he was able. Trial would be in two months.

"Call you first witness. No more motions and stalling," Judge Williams demanded. "I will never understand how the prosecution seems more the defense here!"

"Your honor, the prosecution has never come across anything vaguely like this before," Anne Yolander, prosecutor, replied. "I have studied this case more thoroughly than any case in my career. I don't believe the place for this is in this court. It's in the church across the square.

"I have often decried the professional psychobabblers in court, but this case ... I'm one of them.

"What I'm trying to say...."

"Sum up things at the proper time, or are you the first witness?" Williams said.

"Call Andrew Forbes."

Andy took the stand. He explained that the murders and total information was stipulated, that all was given to the defense. They weren't trying to prove heinous or any such thing. The murders were, actually, not planned by any living person and were not involved with terror or torture or mayhem.

He declared the murders were committed in a time of intense mental confusion and were not the responsibility of the present Marty Harolds.

Yolander led him carefully through the entire investigation and through the things that led him to the solution.

The night of the exorcism was gone through in minute detail. Pictures of the cross burned onto Marty's forehead were shown.

Steve Owens was called as corroborative witness as a break in testimony. The defense did not object and had no questions.

Andy was the only witness for the prosecution. Defense didn't question him, either. Williams stated for the record that he had never held even a minor trial where this kind of thing had happened.

Levin called a well-known psychiatrist to declare he had examined Marty carefully and had found all evidence pointed to a schizoid reaction to a situation for which the patient was conditioned in response for most of his life. He was not responsible for his actions in the murders. His recommendation was to find for mental impairment and for the patient, or prisoner, as used here, be under open observation and treatment. His findings were that the actions would not be repeated.

"Dr. Adkins, you have spoken with the two people present at the so-called exorcism," Levin stated. "My personal feelings are that exorcisms and such are voodoo superstition, yet I find the persons involved to be trustworthy and honest in what they believed happened.

"Will you give a statement of your own beliefs in such ritualistic processes and do you believe this was a successful exorcism?"

"An exorcism depends on the beliefs of several people at once. The exorcist, certainly, and the subject, more certainly.

"This comes under confidentiality laws. I will ask that the courtroom be emptied except for yourself, the jury, the prosecutor, Attorney Levin and arresting officer, Andrew Forbes. Possibly Mr. Owens, as he was present.

"This testimony would be traumatic and negative in impact for the defendant. As his acting physician, I feel it would be better he not be taken through this again. There is no necessity for others involved through no fault of themselves not to be publicly displayed. I will demand the jury be sworn to silence. They must, of course, base their final decisions in some part on the testimony. They must not, ever, discuss it outside the jury room."

There were objections from the reporters and some spectators. Andy had talked with the others involved and the group. They understood this was going to happen and had agreed it was for the best.

When the room was down to the people named, Adkins said he would now answer questions.

"Dr. Adkins, do you believe in possession?"

"No, not in the sense that a demon possesses anyone. That the victim truly believes he is possessed, yes. The actions of a person who is convinced he is possessed are in only the slightest part the responsibility of the victim. The victim actually and truly cannot fight the being he believes is in control of his thoughts and actions."

"Then Mr. Harolds was not actually possessed?"

"It depends upon interpretation of what is a possessor. Yes, he was possessed. Was that possession an outside source? No. Did he have any ability to fight it? No."

"Thank you, doctor, but please do not answer questions that were not asked.

"Did Mr. Harolds have any choice when he committed the murders?"

"No."

"Explain, please?"

"He had been what is commonly termed 'brainwashed' by his mother for his entire life.

She basically ingrained posthypnotic suggestions to be activated by events into him, and she programmed him to cause those situations to arise."

"I don't really know what to ask. Now will be the time to answer questions not asked if you think they are pertinent to this questioning. An essay-form testimony, if you will?"

"Very well.

"Mr. Harolds is, by nature or whatever you want to call it, an affectionate person. He has deep needs to be accepted, yet this is exactly what a monster he called 'Mother' placed to make the responses she had implanted come to fruition. She attached it to the sexual response. She made it appear, and reinforced the idea at any opportunity, that a woman would use his need of affection to entrap him into a life of virtual servitude to her. This is what she was. She projected it to all women. His life was spent with this closest to him.

"He had, for many years, resisted intimate contact because of this deep belief. The time came when he felt his life was wasted because he couldn't allow himself to feel emotionally. He succumbed to the desire for companionship and affection with two women. When it became, as it most obviously must, of sexual content, she was suddenly there, controlling what he did, how he reacted.

"The way he explained it to me, his hands moved of their own volition to strangle those women. His mother was visualized as being there, screeching at him that, see, all women were just what she taught him and he was a no-good bastard pervert for thinking these would be any different.

"She hated men and women. She programmed him to respond to women. He never sought affection from a man before, but she wasn't there to much of an extent and the man he sought contact with was big enough and strong enough to fight her off. Mr. Owens did that, and contacted Detective Forbes, who performed the exorcism.

"This is the part that must not be presented to Mr. Harolds for many years, if ever.

"The exorcism worked because of the programming. Detective Forbes saw what had been done to Mr. Harolds. He was studying the files about it when Mr. Owens called. He went over there, according to his information and to my speaking with him, not knowing what he was going to do, but knowing that Mr. Harolds was not responsible for the murders.

"He did spend some time studying such things

for another case, which he proved was false, and more for this one. He knew it was a psychological control thing. He knew psychological chains were much harder to cut or break than those of mere steel.

"Mr. Harolds was convinced he was headed for Hell without recourse because his father wasn't married to his mother. She had used a line from the old testament to convince him he and to his seventh descendant were doomed when they were born. He considered God to be a sadistic monster because he would so punish the victim and would, as he put it, let the actual sinners off for a couple of hail Marys.

"Forbes first convinced him that such was not the case, that such was refuted. God does not punish the victims. That is to the courts in this country.

"Sorry, but you know why I say that.

"With his convincing, Forbes had the upper hand. The exorcism was a psychological attack against the ideas implanted by the mother. It was a matter of theatrics and display of higher power and knowledge. The subject must be an active part of such actions. Forbes brought him into it to the extent that a cold piece of silver burned an indelible cross into the skin if the believer.

"That tells us that, unquestionably, the exorcism

was a success. Mr. Harolds will not repeat his actions. He is free of that force in his life.

"Who can say if there was an actual demon who was exorcized? It is not important that anyone believe such was the case, *except Mr. Harolds.* For that reason, I asked that he not hear this.

"If there are any questions?"

"You are certain that he is no longer a risk?" Williams asked.

"Absolutely."

"And you will take full responsibility if such proves not to be the case?"

"Ah! I see you are used to professional testifiers who have no real knowledge of such things. In this case, I will."

"Dr. Adkins, do you ask that documentation of this testimony be sealed to insure that Mr. Harolds does not read it?" the court recording secretary asked.

"So ordered," Williams said before Adkins could respond.

"Prosecutor, defense, should this now go to the jury, or would you prefer summation?"

They agreed.

"Bring in the spectators and such."

People filed in. Marty looked a question at Andy. Andy shrugged.

"This will now go to the jury. You have listed

the charges that may be considered and must, to the best of your ability, decide which, if any, will be rendered.

"To the courtroom, the testimony just now taken was of a nature that, quite frankly, is none of anyone's business.

"Court is in recess until jury returns." He banged the gavel.

The jury returned in twenty five minutes. Acts committed while in impaired mental state. Treatment and no imprisonment unless decreed by the presiding judge or the doctor.

Andy and Steve went to talk with Marty. The group came over and said they understood what had happened, to an extent. Mostly, they were supportive of Marty. They hadn't known what kind of absolute Hell he was living in. They would try to make life better for him.

Sarah had come to the trial as a possible prosecution witness. She joined them. They chatted for awhile, then everyone went home.

All-in-all, not too bad.

Marty and Janet ran through the hail of rice to the waiting car. They drove off.

It had been a year and a half since the trial. It took a little while for most to completely forgive Marty. People were naturally suspicious.

He had found affection he so needed. His life had gone from Hell to, if not heaven, at least one of contentment. Janet and he were very well-matched. Both were naturally outgoing affectionate people.

An older man who looked just a bit familiar came to ask Andy if he was the one who had helped Marty so much. Andy said he had done his job, and that Marty wasn't acting on his own volition.

"I know. I'm Silas Gradson, his actual father. From what I managed to learn from TV and the internet, his mother did that to him. I'm one who can testify to that. If I'd known about it, I would've been here in a flash.

"I was never there when he needed me. I thought the man who was supposed to be his father was doing a good job. I should have known that wasn't going to happen. I knew exactly what she was.

"People always said I was strong of mind. I see he is, too. He's a boy any father would be proud of.

"I want to thank you for what you did for my boy. I would have thought that he would be free, no matter what, when she was dead. She managed to be what she was after she was dead."

"Marty once said to me that she was dead, just not quite dead enough," Andy replied. "She is now."

Gradson nodded. "We can hope."

C. D. Moulton's works are available on most major outlets as printed or e-books. CD writes the CD Grimes, PI, mysteries, the Det. Lt. Nick Storie mysteries, the Clint Faraday mysteries, the Flight of the Maita science fiction series, books on orchid culture and many others of many types. Mystery, adventure, intrigue, science fiction, humor, fantasy, paranormal, mild erotica, and factual.